Llama llama and the bully goat

Anna Dewdney

SCHOLASTIC INC.

ISBN 978-0-545-64866-0

12 11 10 9 8 7 6 5 4 3 2 1   13 14 15 16 17 18/0

Printed in China   38

First Scholastic printing, September 2013

Set in ITC Quorum Std
The art for this book was created with oil paint, colored pencil, and oil pastel on primed canvas.

**To my sister Tanya,
with love**

Llama Llama, busy day.
Writing, counting, pictures, clay.

Roll a pancake. Draw the sun.
Almost everyone has fun.

Time for circle. Time for song.
Time to clap and sing along.

Kitty, Rhino, Sheep, and Calf,
Llama, Nelly, and Giraffe
all sing songs in their own way:

moo and *bellow*,
baa and *bray*.

Llama Llama claps the beat.
Gilroy Goat just points and bleats.

Sheep goes *baa* and Calf goes *moo*.
Gilroy thinks that's silly, too.

Llama Llama likes to sing.
Gilroy laughs at **everything.**

Llama sings out just the same.
Gilroy says a not-nice name.

Teacher has some things to say.
Calling names is **not OK**.

Being mean is not allowed.
Teacher says to stop it **now**.

Time for recess!
Go outside.
Monkey bars and
slippy-slides.

Nelly's dolly makes a road.
Fuzzy Llama pulls a load.

Kids climb up
and kids climb down.
Everybody runs around.

Nelly's dolly wants to dig.
Fuzzy drives a great big rig.

Gilroy stands in Fuzzy's way.

Gilroy, do you want to play?

Gilroy bleats and kicks the dirt. He gets sand on Llama's shirt.

Gilroy throws some dirt at Nelly.

Ha ha! Gnus are really smelly!

Gilroy pushes—Fuzzy falls!

Ha ha! Llamas play with dolls!

BULLY

Gilroy, this is **not OK.**
Stop it, or we'll go away.

Being bullied is no fun!

Walk away . . .

and **tell** someone!

Gilroy fusses, frowns, and pouts.

Gilroy gets a
long **time-out.**

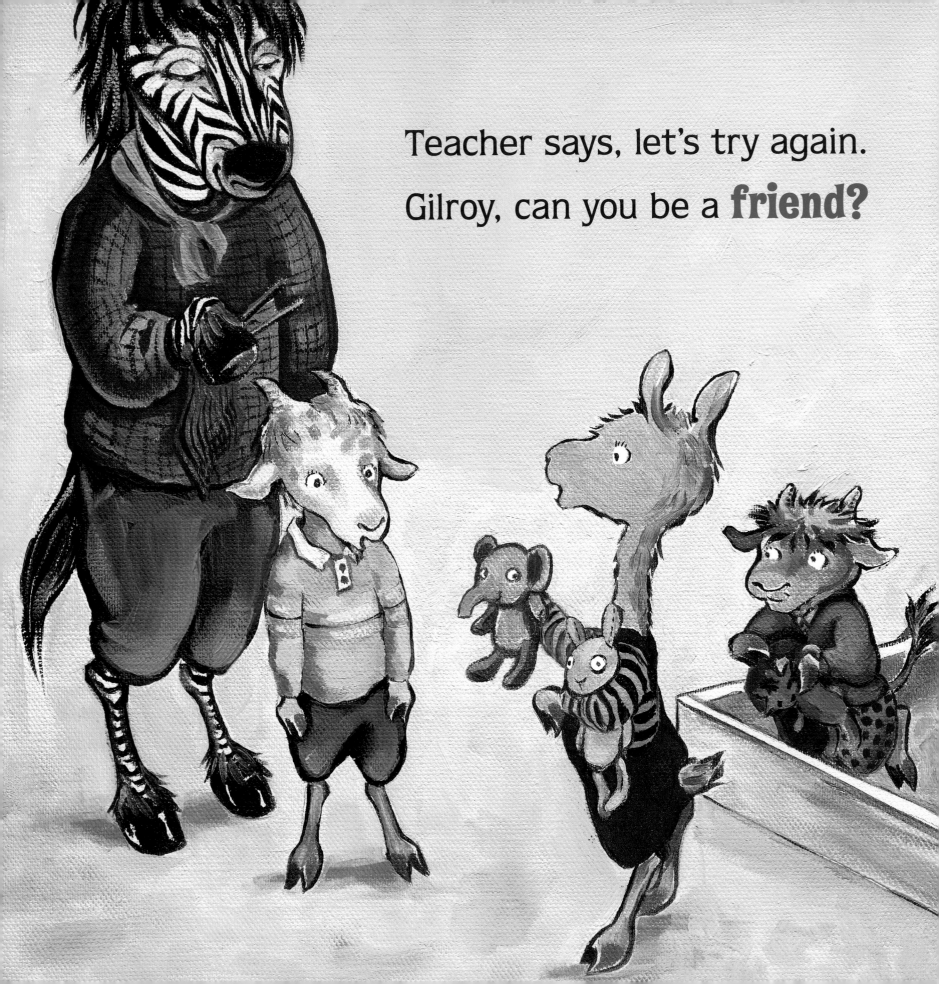

Teacher says, let's try again.

Gilroy, can you be a **friend?**

No more kicking. No more names.
Time to play a nicer game.

End of recess! Back inside.
Gilroy sits by Teacher's side.

Everybody sings the song,
and this time,
Gilroy sings along.

Gilroy Goat has fun with Llama,
but school is over—here comes Mama.

Tomorrow has more games to try. . . .

See you then!

Friends wave good-bye.